The ABC's of NEWS

By Jonathan Harris Miller

Illustrations John McNees

To order additional copies of this book, contact:
Xlibris
844-714-8691
www.Xlibris.com
Orders@Xlibris.com

ISBN: Softcover   978-1-6641-5896-2
        EBook   978-1-6641-5895-5

Print information available on the last page

Rev. date: 03/02/2021

is for Anchor

-- These are the people who report the news to you on TV. They are almost always in a studio.

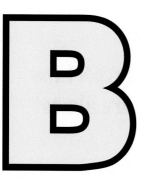

B is for Breaking News

-- No! The news is not actually broken. Breaking News is when brand new information about a story happens.

LIVE

BREAKING

NEWS

bnc

3

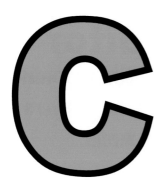

C is for Camera

-- Cameras film the anchors and deliver the show to your TV or device.

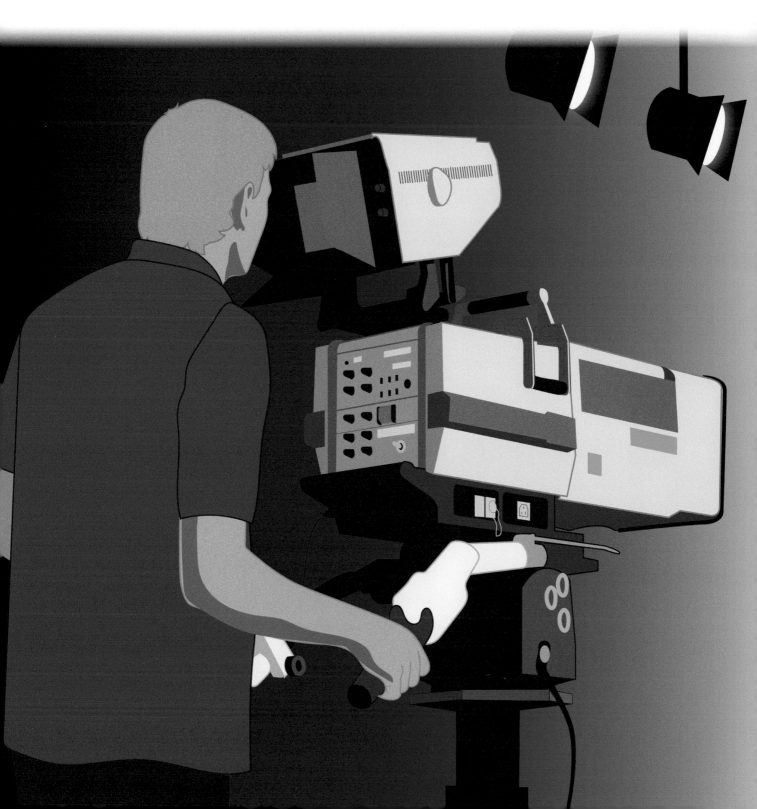

D is for Desk Editor

-- The person at the "desk" edits information. This person finds news stories, answers the phones, and monitors social media.

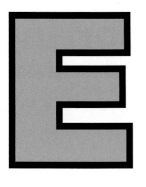

is for Editor

-- Editors are in charge of making what you see on TV look attractive. They "edit" or piece video and sound together to tell a story.

 **is for Field Reporting**

-- Reporting from the field is when someone reports directly from the scene of a story, even in dangerous situations.

 **is for Green Screen**

-- Weather people, or meteorologists, typically stand in front of a "Green Screen" when delivering the forecast. To you, the screen usually appears as a map.

H is for Headline

-- A good headline grabs the viewer's attention. It also summarizes a story in a few words.

LOCAL BOY - JUSTIN T.

bnc 3

LOCAL BOY BRUSHES TEETH ON HIS OWN

is for Investigative Reporting
-- Investigative reporting is when a reporter deeply examines a story to find out all about it. These stories can take years to complete.

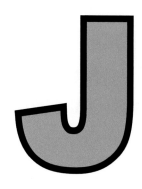

J is for Journalist

-- If you work in the news industry, you are a journalist. Your job is to ask questions and provide people with factually correct information.

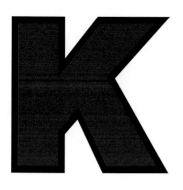

K is for Kicker

-- A "kicker" refers to a story that ends a show. These are usually happier, uplifting stories!

L is for Lead Story

-- The lead story is the first story of a newscast. It grabs your attention because it is important information.

M

is for Meteorologist

-- This person tells us what the weather is going to be so we can plan our day and week.

N is for Newsroom

-- Lots of people work in the newsroom. This is usually a very busy place, especially during breaking news.

O is for "On the Record"

-- This is when a source tells a reporter something they can use as part of a story.

P is for Producer

-- A producer is in charge of putting the show together from beginning to end. This person sits in the control room during a live show and oversees a team of people.

 **is for Questions**
-- Questions are arguably the most important part of working in the news. Asking questions lead to answers which help us give you important information.

R is for Reporter
-- These are the people who collect information and write news stories. They often report from the field and gather information from trusted sources.

**S** **is for Satellite Truck**
-- A satellite truck is filled with technology and a satellite on top that allows reporters in the field to send video or interviews back to the newsroom to be edited.

T is for Teleprompter

-- This is the machine that anchors read from so they can look at you when delivering the news on the TV screen.

U is for Unpredictable
-- Unpredictable things sometimes happen. This is why a newsroom always has to be prepared.

MONKEYS ON HIGHWAY CAUSE
RUSH HOUR MAYHEM

 **is for Voiceover**
-- This is when a reporter records his or her voice to tell a story.

 **is for Who, What, Where, When & Why**

-- These are the five biggest questions a journalist should always consider when writing a story.

 **is for eXciting**

-- Working in the news is always exciting, especially when there is an important election happening.

Y is for Yesterday's News

-- Remember, yesterday's news is old news! There is always something new happening that can be reported and changes the importance and relevance of what happened yesterday.

Z is for Zzzz's

-- Delivering news to you 24 hours a day, 7 days a week is exhausting.

About the Author

Jonathan Harris Miller is a veteran TV news producer based in New York City. Having studied Broadcast & Digital Journalism at the S.I. Newhouse School of Public Communications at Syracuse University, Jonathan believes it's never too early to teach news literacy to young people. His goal in writing this book is to get children excited and interested in news and journalism!

Printed in the United States
By Bookmasters